The Great Elephant

An Illustrated Allegory

Written and Illustrated by Nik Ranieri
Foreword by John MacArthur

WINEPRESS WP PUBLISHING Kids

WinePress Publishing (PO Box 428, Enumclaw, WA 98022) functions only as book publisher. As such, the ultimate design, content, editorial accuracy, and views expressed or implied in this work are those of the author.

ISBN 1-57921-780-X
Library of Congress Catalog Card Number: 2004118351

Printed in Korea

Foreword

In the time-honored and classic style of fables that teach truth, the allegory of the Great Elephant arrives to be added to the treasury of storybooks for teaching children and enriching adults. And the truth beautifully and cleverly rising out of the story is the greatest of all truths—finding the way to God.

Everyone will enjoy the journey in this memorable adventure, and come away not just with entertaining images of the successful quest of a mouse, but with an understanding of the dangers that threaten one's own search for God.

Dr. John MacArthur
Pastor-Teacher, Grace Community Church, Sun Valley, CA
President, The Master's College & Seminary
President, Grace to You Radio
April 19, 2005

Acknowledgments

Jenifer Ranieri, my kids—Jenna, Belle, Quinn, Emily, and Lily, Carol Ranieri, Margaret "Peggy" Holton, Jeff Van Tuyl, Glen Keane, Mark and Marcy Gwinn, John and Patricia MacArthur, Sheila Seifert, and Tony Wilson.

For Jen

Ever since Quinn was a little mouse, he had heard about the Great Elephant. He had even seen evidence of him, but he had never seen him in person. Still he enjoyed listening to the numerous stories that his mom and dad would read to him about the Great Elephant.

They would tell of his long nose and mighty tusks and how he was the biggest creature in all the forest. His dad would also talk of his first meeting with the Great Elephant and how his wisdom and knowledge had helped his dad to survive in the forest these many years. As Quinn grew older, he seemed less interested in the stories—he practically knew them by heart—and more interested in getting out into the world.

The years passed, and eventually Quinn reached the age where it was time for him to leave home and fend for himself. He was excited, but his dad didn't seem to share his enthusiasm.

"Quinn," he said, "the forest is a beautiful place, but it can also be a very dangerous place. Just remember what I've taught you. If you ever get into trouble, seek out the Great Elephant, for he is very wise and knows these woods better than anyone. You need only ask, and he will help you."

"Okay, Dad," said Quinn, only half listening. He really wasn't interested in any help. He was going to prove to his dad that he could make it on his own. Why just yesterday he had scouted out a place a half mile down the river that was the perfect location to settle.

As Quinn was preparing to leave, his mother packed a small bag full of food and other provisions. After a few warm goodbyes, he slung the bag over his shoulder and headed off toward the riverbank.

Quinn hadn't made it very far when it started to rain. This rain was not a typical sun shower. In fact, the drops became so large that it made it difficult for him to go on. Quinn ducked under some leaves to wait out the storm, but an hour later it still hadn't let up.

The sky was dark, and the ground was turning to mud.

"Maybe this wasn't such a good day to start my journey," he thought, deciding that if he had to wait out the storm, he might as well do it in the warmth and comfort of his parents' place. As Quinn turned to head for home, he heard an ominous sound in the distance. It quickly got louder and louder, and before he could react, a torrent of water came flooding toward him.

Afraid for his life, Quinn leapt to the nearest branch and held on tightly. Unfortunately the tree that the branch was attached to succumbed to the pull of the water and was carried down toward the river with Quinn hanging on for dear life.

"HELP!" he cried, but his voice was drowned out by the sound of the powerful rapids. The river twisted and turned, carrying Quinn for miles. Then just as he thought he wouldn't be able to hold on any longer, the tree suddenly lodged in the muddy edge of the river and jolted to a stop. The branch that Quinn had been clinging to snapped off and both went flying over the riverbank and into a patch of wet leaves.

Quinn was shaken but relieved that he was still in one piece. He looked around.
He didn't know this part of the forest at all.

Quinn tried to find shelter for the night, but all the burrows were either filled with water or had been collapsed by the flood. He saw a patch of dirt a few feet away that looked dry, but upon checking, it turned out to be quicksand. It seemed that his every attempt to find comfort ended in failure.

He sat at the edge of a shallow ditch—cold, tired and afraid. Through some small miracle, he had managed to hold on to the small bag that his mother had packed, but contained only a few days' rations. Quinn didn't know what to do. He couldn't go ome. He didn't even know where home was.

Quinn was completely at a loss as to what to do next. He glanced around to try and get his bearings and that was when he realized there was something odd about this ditch. He looked up and saw several more heading off into the distance. Why, they weren't ditches at all. In fact, they looked like something he had seen when he was very young. His eyes widened.

"The Great Elephant," he exclaimed. "That's it! I'll find the Great Elephant. He'll help me!"

Quinn began to follow the tracks carefully, but after several minutes, he started to feel uncomfortable. The forest was quiet—a little too quiet. As he quickened his pace, he heard a rustling in the bushes, and before he knew it, a huge snake was blocking the path.

"Please, don't eat me!" he cried.

"Eat you?" replied the snake. "Why, nothing could be farther from my mind!"

"But I thought, uh...well, my dad always said that snakes ate mice."

"Oh for heaven snake! I bet he also told you that I'm mean, have sharp fangs speak with a forked tongue..."

"Yes, that's right," agreed Quinn.

"...and that I love to help others," continued the Snake.

"I hadn't heard that."

"Of course not! Only the bad stuff, none of the good. Lies! All lies! Oh, th stories these fathers tell to their children!" moaned the snake. "I hear it all th time from misguided forest creatures just like you."

"Do you really help others?" Quinn asked suspiciously.

"Yes, let me prove it to you. Tell me where you're headed."

Quinn paused to study him. He was quite an attractive snake, not at all like the scary creature his father had described. Perhaps it would be all right to confide in him.

"Well," he began, "I'm lost, and I need to find the Great Elephant."

"Fangtastic!" exclaimed the snake. "He's a good friend of mine. "Y'know, if you keep going the way you're going, it'll take you forever to find him. I know a shortcut. Head down this other path, and it should lead you right to him."

Quinn looked at both paths. Even though the one he was traveling on still had the footprints, it was starting to narrow a bit, while the path that the snake recommended seemed a little wider and a lot more inviting. Quinn was feeling a little anxious, so any suggestion that would help him reach his goal faster was welcome.

After thanking the snake for his help, he proceeded along the wider path. He felt better about the snake and wondered why his dad had said such unkind things about him. After all, he had been extremely helpful.

As he continued along the path, he noticed the prints dried in the mud that belonged to other animals. One set resembled elephant prints, but they didn't look as big. Perhaps the floodwaters had shrunk them. Quinn followed the prints until they eventually led him to a creature with a long nose and a pair of tusks. Quinn could not conceal his excitement.

"Are you the Great Elephant?

"Who, me?" spouted a very muddy warthog. "Oh no, no, no, of course not. Well...not yet."

"What do you mean, 'not yet'?" asked Quinn.

"You've heard of the Great Elephant's fine tusks and long snout, haven't you?" replied the warthog. Quinn nodded, and the warthog continued, "Do not my fine tusks and my long snout slightly resemble his? Someday I'll be just like him."

The warthog's words seemed odd to Quinn.

"You know," said the warthog, "your ears resemble those of the Great Elephant. Someday you could become like him as well." Quinn's brow furrowed. If the warthog were right, that would mean the Great Elephant was once a different animal. Quinn didn't remember any of his dad's stories mentioning that.

"Hey," said the warthog. "I'm on my way to see the Great Elephant too. Why don't you follow me? I know he'll be happy that I brought a friend along, especially one that shows such potential."

Quinn considered the warthog's offer, but the idea that a small mouse could ever be as big as the Great Elephant was something just too unbelievable. Besides, based on what the warthog said, Quinn had little hope that the warthog would lead him to the real Great Elephant. He really didn't want to take any chances, so he graciously declined and hurried on his way.

The sun was setting, and the night wind sent a chill up Quinn's back. He knew that soon he would have to stop and rest for the night. By the side of the trail, he noticed a warm light shining from a hole in a tree. Quinn climbed the trunk to find that the lights were really two eyes.

"Whoo are you, and what do you want?" asked a large owl stepping out from the shadows. Quinn's pulse quickened as he recalled what his dad had told him about owls and their appetite for mice.

"I- I'm just looking for a place to stay for the night b- before I continue on my journey to find the Great Elephant," he stammered.

The owl started to laugh, and Quinn felt the tension ease a little. "Oh no not another one," sighed the owl. "You poor deluded creature, there is no such animal!"

"But how can you be sure?" asked Quinn.

"Well, it's really quite logical; I've never seen him," retorted the owl. "And if I haven't seen him, he must not exist. Besides, if there ever were such a creature, he's probably been dead for centuries."

Quinn was skeptical.

"It's all here in black and white," continued the owl. "As you can see, I have dozens of excellent books on the subject."

Quinn browsed through the titles. "But all these books are written by you," he exclaimed.

"Of course! After all I am the wisest animal in the forest," gloated the pompous bird. "Feel free to read through them while I'm gone, and I'm sure you'll discover for yourself what an enormous waste of time your search would be." The owl stepped out of the knothole and spread his wings. "Well, I'm off to dinner," he said. "There's this swamp about a half a mile north of here that's just teaming with large prey."

"Whew, for a moment there, I thought that you were going to eat me."

The owl laughed. "I need a *meal*, not an appetizer. You are welcome to rest here."

Quinn breathed a sigh of relief as he watched the bird fly off into the night. Settling into the knot in the tree, Quinn tried to make sense of this new information. The owl was known throughout the forest for his great intelligence, but was the Great Elephant a myth? Were his father's stories just fables? Could those footprints he had followed been a faint reminder of a time long ago when the Great Elephant did roam the forest? Quinn's mind was racing, but eventually fatigue caught up with him, and without a single question answered, he fell fast asleep.

As the sun rose early the next day, Quinn felt a sharp jab in his side.

"Are you alive or dead?" asked a deep voice.

Quinn cracked one eye open. The morning light silhouetted the figure hovering over him.

"Huh, what?" responded Quinn groggily.

"Oh, you are alive!" said the voice.

Quinn opened both eyes. This was not the owl talking to him but a very inquisitive vulture. He was surprised by the bird's appearance, for he had heard that vultures were mangy and scrawny, but this one was sharply groomed and looked to be very well fed.

"What did the owl do—chew you up and spit you out?" questioned the bird.

"Well I sort of feel that way after talking to him," Quinn replied. "You see, I told him that I was looking for the Great Elephant, and he told me that there was no such animal. He told me that I was silly and to forget the whole thing."

"Oh, don't listen to him," snuffed the vulture. "He won't believe in anything unless it's staring him right in the face."

"But he sounded logical," said Quinn.

"Is it logical that anyone who sleeps during the day and is awake at night, would see much of anything?" countered the bird. "Besides, you happen to be looking a someone who has not only seen the Great Elephant but knows him personally."

Quinn perked up. "You know the Great Elephant? Can you tell me where I can find him?" he asked.

"Of course, I will tell you all I know," he paused, "for a price. You see, I've worked long and hard to gain this knowledge, and I just can't give it away for free."

"But I really don't have anything of value," said the mouse. "All I have is this small bag of provisions."

"Give till it hurts, my boy," responded the vulture. "Knowledge of the Great Elephant doesn't come cheap."

Quinn opened up his sack, pulled out a small piece of food and handed it over to the vulture. As the vulture took the morsel, he began to describe the Great Elephant in detail.

"The Great Elephant glows like the sun!" said the bird. "He is *wealthy* in knowledge and *rich* in power."

"Wow, he seems so lofty. I wonder if he would even see me," said Quinn.

"Well, I just happen to be his closest advisor," replied the vulture. "Just tell him I sent you."

"Where do I find him? How will I recognize him? Please tell me more," begged Quinn.

The vulture eyed Quinn's sack and spoke only when Quinn offered him more things from it. Soon, Quinn had not only lost his provisions, but he'd lost his shirt as well. Finally, the vulture finished talking and spread his wings to leave.

"Wait, you haven't even told me how to find him," said Quinn exasperated.

"I'm sorry, my boy," said the vulture as he flew off. "The Great Elephant won't see anyone who shows up empty-handed."

Quinn was panicked. Not only was he lost and alone, but now he had no food left. He began frantically running along the path, watching the ground for any signs that the Great Elephant had traveled this way.

All of a sudden, he bumped into someone. Quinn looked up, and to hi surprise saw another mouse—only this mouse was bigger than any mouse Quin had ever seen.

"Oh, I'm sorry I bumped into you, but, I guess if I had to bump into someone I'm glad it was a family member. You are a mouse, aren't you?"

"First of all, you nee to keep your eyes on th road, son," admonishe the large rodent, "and I'r hardly a family membe I'm a rat, more like a lon lost relative—a distan cousin—twice removed."

"Well, cousin," said Quinn, "maybe you can help me. I'm searching for the Great Elephant."

"My son," spoke the rat softly, "you don't need to go any farther. The Great Elephant will be visiting me very shortly—immediately—within the hour."

"So you've seen him?" inquired Quinn.

"Many times, hundreds of times, thousands even," responded the rat as he led Quinn into his home. "Come, wait with me, and I'll tell you all about it."

"This isn't going to cost me anything, is it?" Quinn asked suspiciously.

"Of course not. Besides you don't have anything to give. Still, this room could use some tidying up—dusting, general cleaning. The Great Elephant won't show up unless this place is spotless."

Quinn grabbed a broom and went to work. The rat even gave him a snack t
"keep up his strength." As Quinn worked, the rat began to read stories about th
Great Elephant. While listening, he noticed that although the description of th
Great Elephant was familiar, there was something not quite right about it.

"These don't sound like the stories my dad used to read to me," said Quinn.

"Yes, well, those stories happened so long ago," retorted the rat. "These are new, up-to-date stories, sequels, new chapters to an old tale."

"But the Great Elephant sounds different in your stories," Quinn replied. "I mean, you haven't even mentioned his mighty tusks."

"Tusks!" balked the rat. "Don't be ridiculous! You could poke someone's eye out with one of those. The Great Elephant loves everyone. He would never need such crude appendages." The rat gestured toward the corner of the room. "You've missed a spot." Quinn went back to work hoping that the Great Elephant would show up soon, but by nightfall there was still no sign of him. Eventually, Quinn was so exhausted that he fell asleep while scrubbing the floor.

Early the next morning, Quinn woke up to the sound of the rat snoring. As he looked around, he was shocked to discover that the place didn't look any cleaner. The rat had already messed up the areas that Quinn had cleaned. All his work had been a complete waste of time. Quinn was pretty upset that he had spent most of yesterday here, and he certainly didn't want to spend any more time cleaning up after that sloppy rat! Besides, the Great Elephant that he was looking for was not the one in the rat's stories. So, while the rat slept, Quinn left to continue his search.

After a few hours of following the trail, Quinn grew frustrated. He seemed no closer to his goal than he had been two days ago. He had heard so many different views, versions, and ideas of the Great Elephant that he didn't know what to think. Still, he was determined not to let anything or anyone delay him further from finding the Great Elephant.

Unfortunately, a few minutes later he was stopped in his tracks once again. The path unexpectedly split into several smaller paths, each heading in a different direction. Quinn slumped down in the middle of the trail.

"Now what am I going to do?" he cried.

As he stared at the paths, out of the corner of his eye, he noticed a wolf lying in the grass, half concealed by the shade of a tree. Normally he would have been afraid, but now everything seemed so hopeless that he didn't even care.

"Problem?" asked the wolf.

"Yeah, I'm lost," said Quinn dejectedly. "All I've been trying to do for the last few days is find the Great Elephant. Everyone I've met along the way has had all these different ideas and stories about him. The rat says that he knows the Great Elephant. The warthog said that he was going to become the Great Elephant. The owl said that the Great Elephant didn't exist, and the vulture, well, I have no idea what he was talking about. I just don't know who or what to believe anymore."

"The solution is simple," said the wolf. "They're all correct. You see, everyone speaks of him in different ways, but they all still call him the Great Elephant. And it doesn't matter which one of these paths you take. They all lead to him."

Quinn shook his head. He couldn't believe what he was hearing. "That's just ridiculous. They can't *all* be right!"

The wolf laughed wickedly. Suddenly out from the bushes stepped the wart hog. Then out popped the vulture, followed by the rat, the owl, and finally the snake. Quinn gasped as the animals surrounded him.

"So, my boy, no luck in finding the Great Elephant along this path, eh? Didn' I mention that this was a dead end?" hissed the snake. "This should be a lesson to you about taking advice from strangers."

The other animals laughed. "You see, I have a confession to make. I lied. I do eat mice. I just like to start out by playing with my food a little. Well done, my friends. You shall be rewarded handsomely for your efforts."

"I get the next one!" squawked the vulture.

Quinn shut his eyes waiting for the inevitable. Suddenly he felt the ground shake. All the animals looked up to see the forest react to the swelling vibration.

A split second later the Great Elephant ripped through the brush, dividing it like a cloth being torn in two. He charged toward the terrified group of animals and with his long and powerful trunk, reached into the midst of them and lifted Quinn into the air and out of harm's way. The animals on the ground scurried like cockroaches. But as hard as they tried, they could not escape the enormous feet of the elephant and were trampled into the dirt.

When the dust cleared, the animals were gone. Quinn was stunned and for a moment unable to speak.

"I... I found you!" he blurted out.

The Great Elephant smiled. "Actually, I found you."

"But how? I mean, I took the wrong path, and I was completely surrounded by all those animals."

"I think I have a slightly higher vantage point than most animals," responded the wise elephant.

Quinn smiled with a feeling of both joy and relief as he stood in the presence of this awesome creature. He wanted to ask for help, but he felt a little embarrassed.

"All I wanted to do was to strike out on my own," Quinn said timidly. "But I guess I wasn't fully prepared for the hazards of the forest."

"Quinn, it's a jungle out there," said the Great Elephant as he began to walk through the woods with Quinn riding on the top of his head. "And some take longer than others to realize that they need help."

Quinn was quiet for a moment. Then he looked around.

"Where are we going?"

"To start your new life," said the elephant.

"Are you taking me back to the place I chose by the bank of the river?" asked Quinn.

42

"No," said the Great Elephant. "That place was destroyed by the storm."

When the Great Elephant finally stopped, Quinn immediately recognized the thick bushes and quicksand. It was the place where he had first started his quest. He wondered why they were here, but he trusted the elephant and waited to see what would happen next.

The Great Elephant placed Quinn on the ground and with his mighty tusks he cleared away the offending trees and bushes, allowing the light to shine through.

Next he pushed dirt over the quicksand and pounded it into solid ground with his powerful feet.

Finally he picked up a rock with his sturdy trunk and lodged it in the dirt providing a solid foundation for Quinn's house. Quinn couldn't believe his eyes All his life he had heard about the Great Elephant, but he had never seemed a real to him as he did at this very moment. He was just as his dad had described him—in appearance and in deed.

After the work was complete, the Great Elephant did not leave. He stayed with Quinn and talked with him until Quinn's eyes were opened to the ways of th forest. Once Quinn was sufficiently settled in his new surroundings, the Grea Elephant knew it was time to be on his way.

"Quinn," he said. "When you need me, you know how to find me. Just follow the footprints."

Quinn understood and assured the Great Elephant that he would let others especially those who looked lost, know about the footprints. And he would te how the Great Elephant delivered him from the jaws of death.

44

As the Great Elephant prepared to leave, Quinn looked up at him and asked,
"You won't forget about me, will you?"

The Great Elephant knelt down, smiled, and softly responded, "Quinn, an
lephant never forgets."

THE END

A Note from the Author

In today's society, tolerance is taught as a virtue and indeed it is. Being tolerant of other people's interests and preferences shows patience and love. But when it comes to error and fallacy, do we tolerate or accept it? Not according to the Bible which is the ultimate authority on right and wrong—especially when it's the Word of God that is being misrepresented. We are called to ". . . be ready to *give* a defense . . . for the hope that is in you" (1 Peter 3:15).

There is a trend nowadays that is pushing for all the world's religions to get together, after all, "we're all working towards the same goal." This philosophy obviously comes from people who have very little faith in their own beliefs or from those secular individuals who see religion as man made. To compromise the Christian faith in that way is to ignore the many statements of exclusivity that are found in the Scriptures.

Because not all are drawn to the false deities of other religions, Satan at his most deceptive has led many to pervert the truth so as to deceive many more. These "cults" have distorted, replaced, or just totally thrown out life saving truths and have concealed their blasphemy under the umbrella of Christianity (2 Timothy 4:3-4). The cults are under the assumption that the Bible has been tampered with. But to conclude that man could somehow corrupt our only link to salvation is to say that God is not in total control (2 Timothy 3:16; Matthew 5:18).

Whether through historical events, lofty ideals or prophetical writings, the Bible and only the Bible, proves itself to be inerrant, reliable, and a firm foundation with which to stand on.

This book attempts to show, rather obviously, that when you ignore or change some of the truth, all is compromised, turning it into "quite a different animal."

Nik Ranieri, December 2004

To order additional copies of

The Great Elephant

Have your credit card ready and call

Toll free: (877) 421-READ (7323)

or send $19.95* each plus $5.95 S&H** to

WinePress Publishing
PO Box 428
Enumclaw, WA 98022

or order online at: www.winepressbooks.com

*Washington residents, add 8.4% sales tax

**add $1.50 S&H for each additional book ordered